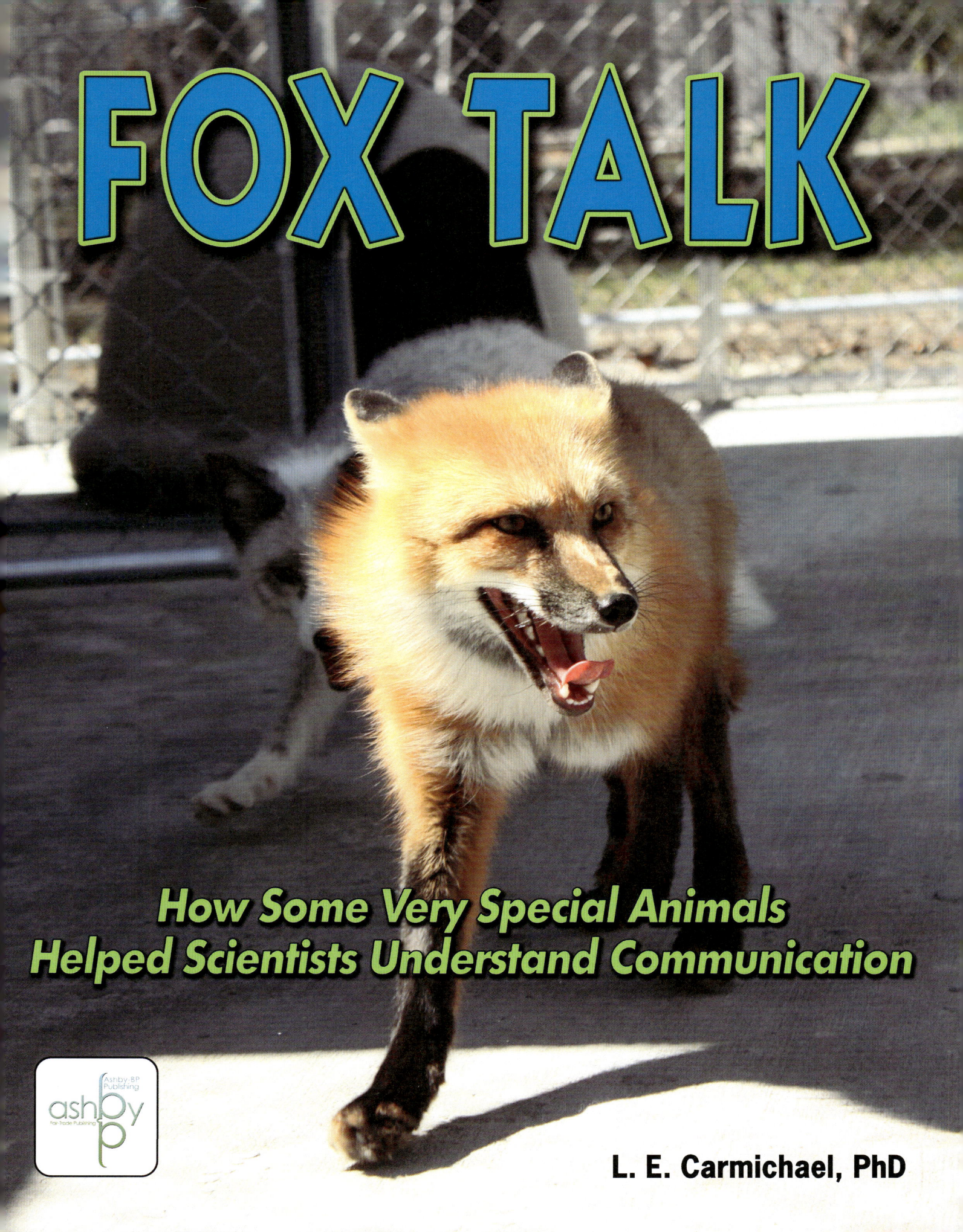

FOX TALK

How Some Very Special Animals Helped Scientists Understand Communication

L. E. Carmichael, PhD

ACKNOWLEDGMENTS

It took a whole team of people to make my book look this good. Thanks to my critique group, Kate Lacy, Halli Lilburn, Antje Martens-Oberwelland, and Ishta Mercurio, for cheerleading and scolding, as required. To Helaine Becker and Joan Marie Galat, thank you for sharing your experience, expertise, and enthusiasm. And props to my editor, Karen Latchana Kenney, for smoothing the edges and pointing out the bits that didn't make sense. If any are left, it's my fault for not listening.

Special thanks to the scientists who shared their knowledge (and their photos!): Svetlana Gogoleva, Brian Hare, Anna Kukekova, Adam Miklosi, François Valla, and Ilya Volodin. Thanks to Renée Baker and Mitchel Kalmanson, and to Carol and Robert Price, for giving me the opportunity to meet their foxes, and to Matthew, Amelia, and Oliva for being such great models. The book wouldn't be the same without you.

To my family and friends, for their unflagging support: I couldn't have done it without you. And to my partner in both crime and puppy love, thank you for bringing me food when I'm on deadline.

*For my Dad, who's run out of buttons to burst,
and for my Mom,
who would have loved to pet the foxes*

TABLE OF CONTENTS

CHAPTER 1

CANINE COMMUNICATION

When you talk to a dog, does the dog talk back? Many people think so.

Scientist Anna Kukekova says, "Without a word from them, we understand our dogs very well. We can read their body language, facial expressions, habits, and emotional states, and they can read ours. They can understand our mood, intent, tone of voice, and words from our language."

Dogs and people share information with each other. This communication is a mystery scientists wanted to solve. They started by asking how dogs became man's best friend.

Using communication, a boy teaches his puppy to sit.

Speaking Human

Big or small, short or tall, every dog's ancestors were wolves. Thousands of years ago, these wolves lived in packs. They used sounds, smells, and body language to communicate with other wolves.

Then something new happened. A few wolves began to spend time around human villages. They stole food people had thrown away. Over time, the wolves' descendants changed. They became less scared of humans. Eventually, the wolves turned into a new species— dogs. This is the process of domestication.

Wolves communicate with sounds and body language.

FURRY FRIENDS

Most dogs come from Middle Eastern wolves that lived around 15,000 years ago. In 1978, scientists found a grave in Israel, a country in the Middle East. The grave was 12,000 years old. It held the bones of a person and a dog puppy. To be buried together, they must have had a very special bond.

Jordan is another country in the Middle East. In a grave in Jordan, scientists found two people buried with fox bones. Like the dog puppy, scientists believe this fox was a special pet.

Domestication is a special type of evolution. It changes animals from being wild to being tame. Wild animals hide from people or try to attack them. Tame animals like to be around people.

Snarling means a wolf is about to attack.

Dogs, wolves, and foxes are part of the canine family of mammals. Because they are relatives, their appearance and behavior are similar.

A pug puppy leans in to give his girl a kiss.

Like wolves, dogs communicate with others in their pack. But a dog's pack is made up of people. People cannot prick their ears or wag their tails. They cannot speak using smells. They use words instead of howls and growls.

So how did dogs learn to speak human? Scientists still did not know, because the change happened so long ago. But maybe foxes—dogs' canine cousins—could help answer this question.

There are many domestic species besides dogs. These include:
cats
guinea pigs
horses
cows
sheep
chickens

CHAPTER 2

BELYAEV'S AMAZING EXPERIMENT

DNA is a molecule in living things. It affects the way animals look and behave.

Like all kinds of evolution, domestication changes a species' DNA. These changes can alter animals' size, fur color, or tail shape. They can also alter how animals behave around people.

Russian scientist Dmitri Belyaev believed that behavior was the most important difference between wolves and dogs. After all, wolves avoid people, but dogs want to lick peoples' faces. To find out how domestication changes behavior, Belyaev designed an amazing experiment.

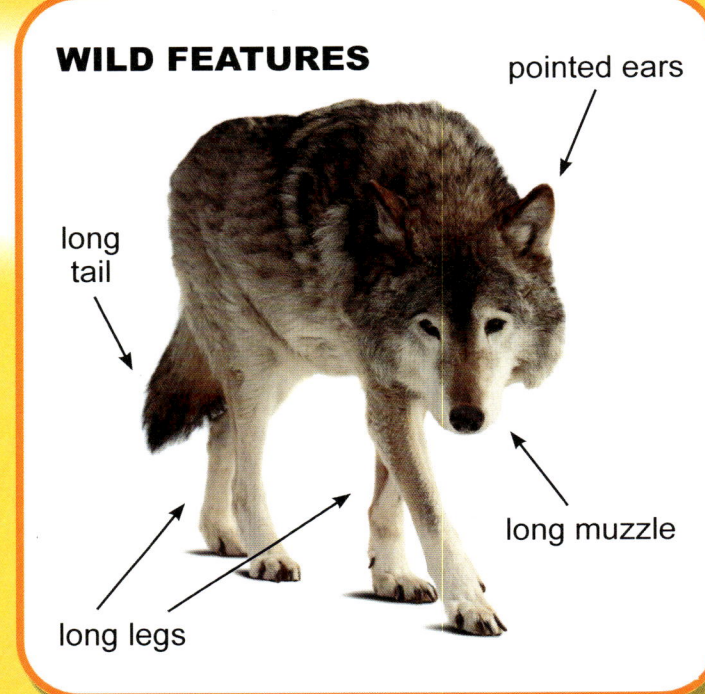

WILD FEATURES

pointed ears

long tail

long muzzle

long legs

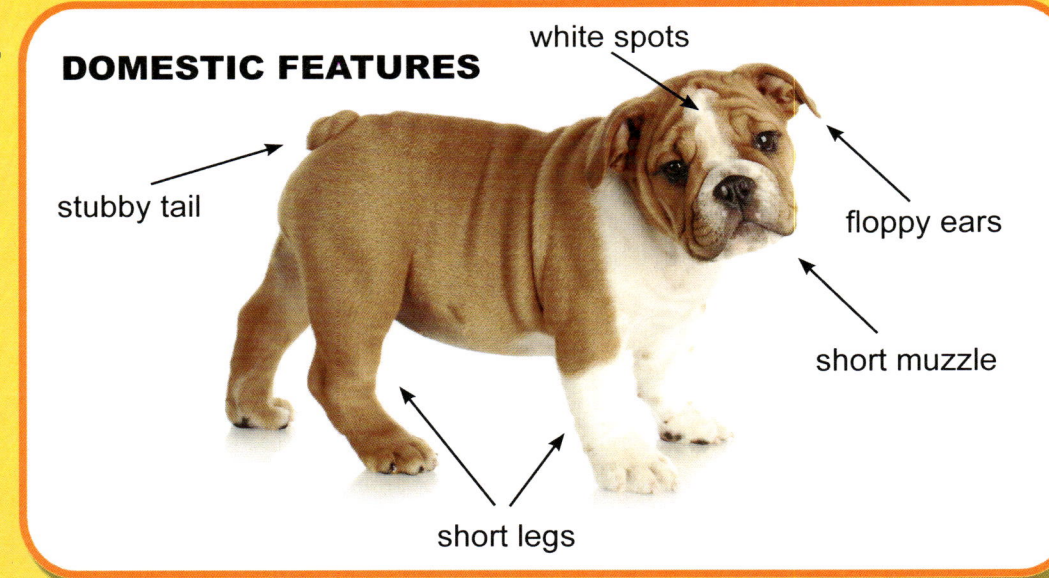

DOMESTIC FEATURES

white spots

stubby tail

floppy ears

short muzzle

short legs

Dog domestication took thousands of years. Belyaev would try to speed up this process. He would try to turn wild red foxes into tame ones. If it worked, scientists could watch as changes occurred. They could use these special foxes to understand communication.

To learn about dogs, it made sense to study foxes. They are both part of the canine family, so they have a lot in common. Belyaev believed that meant the foxes, if domesticated, would be similar to dogs.

Belyaev's second reason was that red foxes already lived around people. In Russia, foxes were raised and sold for their valuable fur. But these foxes were not tame. People could not touch them without danger of being bitten. The foxes lived on farms, but their behavior was wild.

Dmitri Belyaev and three of his domesticated foxes. This photo was taken in Russia in 1984, twenty-five years after the experiment started.

RED FOXES

Wild red foxes live in more places than almost any other land animal. They are found in Canada, the United States, northern Asia, and most of Europe.

Despite their name, not all red foxes have red fur. About 10 percent have dark gray or black fur, and some are even white.

The Experiment Begins

In 1959, Belyaev's team of scientists bought 130 farm foxes to start the experiment. Each fox had its own wire cage at the Institute of Cytology and Genetics in Siberia, Russia. The scientists were not allowed to pet the foxes or train them. Training changes an animal's behavior. To study domestication, Belyaev's team needed to see DNA changes only. Training would ruin the experiment.

DOMESTIC OR TRAINED?

Circus lions and animal actors are trained to be gentle around people. But training does not change their DNA, so their babies are still wild. Domestic animals have different DNA than their wild ancestors. Their babies will also be domestic.

Aggressive foxes flatten their ears to show anger towards people.

Above: This farm fox is not domesticated. It is trying to get away from the person taking its picture. Below: Domestic foxes are relaxed and happy around people.

To measure behavior, the scientists tested the foxes' reactions to people. They needed to answer several questions. Did the fox stand at the front of its cage, or did it hide at the back? Did the fox growl or snarl? Were its ears relaxed, or pinned to the side of its head? Would the fox let people touch it, or try to bite? The team took notes on each of the foxes. The notes showed how wild foxes behaved at the beginning of the experiment.

Belyaev's team chose the tamest foxes for breeding. Only one fox out of every ten was chosen. After the foxes mated, they had puppies. The scientists tested how the puppies behaved around people. Then the breeding cycle started again.

LEARNING FEAR

When animals are born, they cannot feel fear. They learn to be afraid of new things as they grow. Fear helps them avoid dangers in the wild.

Wolves and wild foxes learn fear when they are one-and-a-half months old. Domestic foxes don't learn fear until they are four months old. Dogs take up to six months. Scientists call the time before fear the socialization period. It is longer in domestic animals than in wild ones. This gives domestic animals extra time to learn that people can be part of their packs.

A domestic fox puppy at the Institute of Cytology and Genetics, in Russia.

By 2009, around 50,000 foxes had been born as part of Belyaev's experiment.

Becoming Tame

The results were surprising. Fox behavior changed much faster than scientists expected. After just three rounds of breeding, fox puppies stopped trying to attack people. After four rounds, a fox puppy wagged its tail like a happy dog. No fox had ever wagged at a person before.

Today, after 50 years of breeding, the wild foxes have become domesticated. When domestic foxes see people, they whine and wiggle for attention. They nibble people's fingers and slurp people's faces. They take walks on leashes and come when they're called. Puppies do these things when they're just three weeks old, too young to know very much about people.

Arsi, a domestic fox, gives his human friend a kiss. Arsi is wearing a harness that connects to a leash.

Team member Anna Kukekova says, "They remind me a lot of golden retrievers, who are basically not aware that there are good people, bad people, people that they have met before, and those they haven't."

The foxes' DNA had changed. The next step was to see if the foxes could talk.

Two girls play with a golden retriever.

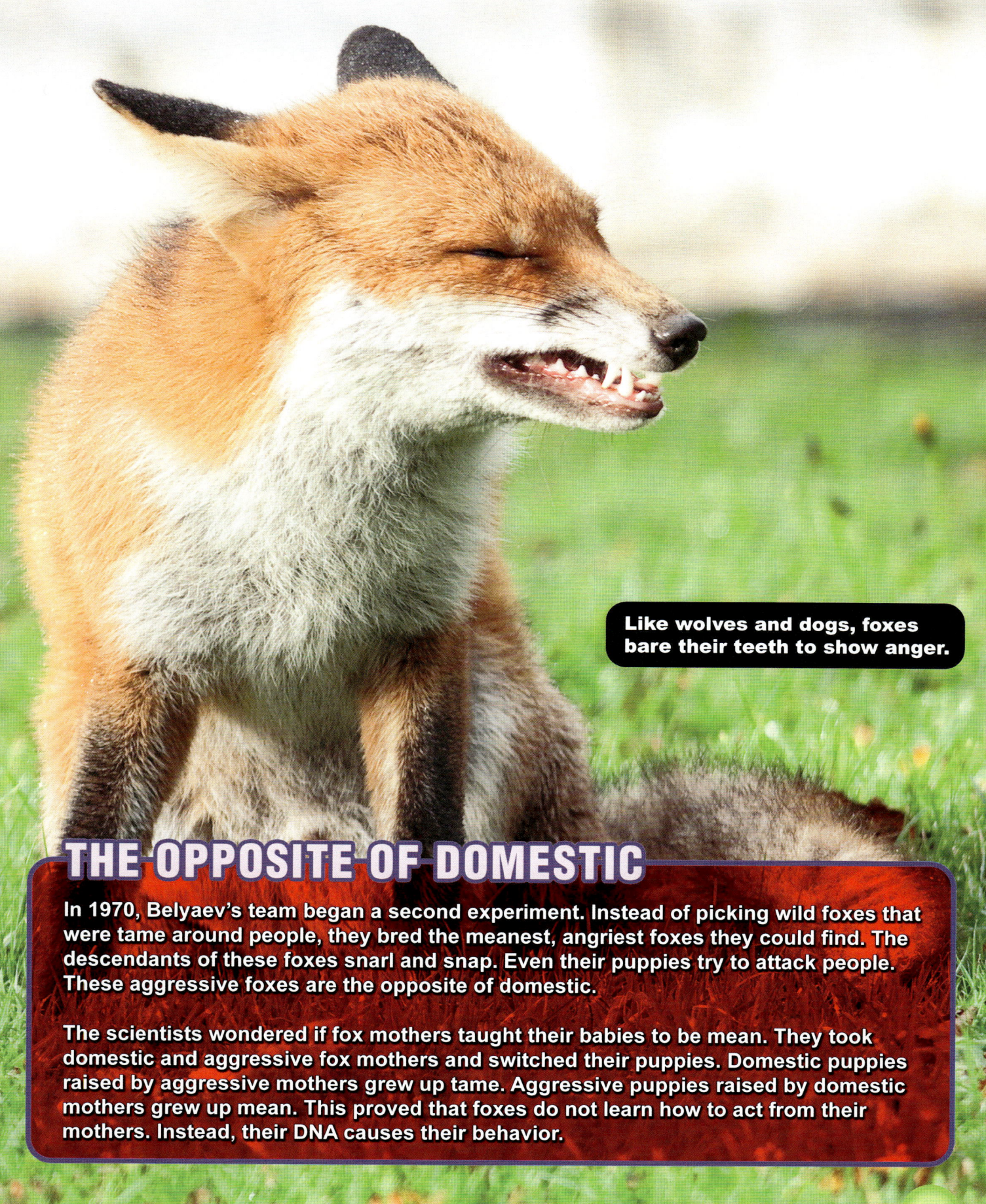

Like wolves and dogs, foxes bare their teeth to show anger.

THE OPPOSITE OF DOMESTIC

In 1970, Belyaev's team began a second experiment. Instead of picking wild foxes that were tame around people, they bred the meanest, angriest foxes they could find. The descendants of these foxes snarl and snap. Even their puppies try to attack people. These aggressive foxes are the opposite of domestic.

The scientists wondered if fox mothers taught their babies to be mean. They took domestic and aggressive fox mothers and switched their puppies. Domestic puppies raised by aggressive mothers grew up tame. Aggressive puppies raised by domestic mothers grew up mean. This proved that foxes do not learn how to act from their mothers. Instead, their DNA causes their behavior.

CHAPTER 3

BODY TALK

When you drop food on the floor, how do you show a dog where to find it?

Probably, you point. The dog then looks in the direction you are pointing. Dogs do not point, because they do not have fingers. So how do they know what pointing means?

Scientists thought there were two possibilities. Dogs may learn what pointing means by watching people. Or maybe all dogs understand pointing because of domestication. If that is true, domestic foxes should understand pointing, too.

Hunting Hidden Food

In 2003, American scientist Brian Hare and his team tested fox puppies with an object-choice experiment. This test used fox treats and two bowls. One scientist held the fox. A second scientist hid food in one bowl. Then he put both bowls on the floor, 1.5 meters (4.9 feet) apart. The scientist pointed to the bowl that hid the food. If the fox picked the correct bowl, it got to eat the treat.

Scientists measured how many times the fox got it right. If the fox did not understand pointing, it guessed. Guessing gives the right answer about 50 percent of the time. Foxes that understood pointing found the food more than 50 percent of the time.

Hare's team compared six domestic fox puppies with six wild fox puppies. Domestic foxes chose the correct bowl more often than wild foxes. That meant domestic foxes were better at using information from pointing. The foxes were doing more than finding food. They were communicating with the scientists.

Testing communication using an object-choice experiment.

Some scientists believe foxes go towards human hands because they expect food or petting.

WOLVES, DOGS, AND FOXES, TOO

Wolves live in the wild. Most dogs live with people. How could scientists tell if dogs were better communicators? Dogs have more chances to learn from people. Comparing wolves to dogs is not fair.

This dog puppy is just a few days old. It needs constant care to survive.

In 2008, scientists in Hungary solved this problem. They started an experiment with dog and wolf puppies that were four to ten days old. Each puppy was given to a person. These people fed and cared for their puppies 24 hours a day. Because of this, the wolves thought people were pack members. They were not scared of humans.

When the puppies were four months old, scientists did an object-choice experiment. Dogs found the hidden food 70 percent of the time. Wolves got the right answer only 50 percent of the time. The wolves were not communicating with people—they were guessing.

The scientists found that extra training helped the wolves communicate. Dog puppies did not need this training. Six-week-old dog puppies were as good at communicating as adult dogs. Unlike wolves, dogs are born knowing how to communicate with people.

In a different experiment, Brian Hare compared fox puppies to dog puppies. He discovered that domestic foxes found as much food as dogs did. This was extra proof that domestication helps animals communicate.

This fox puppy is the same age as the ones Brian Hare used in his experiments.

A girl communicates with a domestic fox.

Domestic foxes are not trained. They have no chance to learn the meaning of pointing. Because of this, Hare knew that communication came from domestication.

This is extra amazing, because Belyaev's team did not choose foxes for their brains. "They didn't select for a smarter fox but for a nice fox," Hare explains. "But they ended up getting a smart fox."

Foxes that like people are better at communicating with people. The same is true for dogs.

AT-HOME EXPERIMENT: DOES YOUR DOG COMMUNICATE?

You can try your own animal experiment at home.
To find out if your dog understands pointing, you will need:

- ◆ Two bowls
- ◆ Dog treats
- ◆ A friend to help

Follow these steps:

- ◆ Put a treat in one bowl and let your dog eat it.
  This teaches the dog that food is hidden in the bowls.
- ◆ Ask your friend to hold your dog until you are ready.
- ◆ Stand 2 meters (6.6 feet) in front of your dog.
- ◆ Hide a treat in one bowl. Make sure your dog does not see!
- ◆ Put the bowls on the floor, 1.5 meters (4.9 feet) apart.
- ◆ Point toward the correct bowl, using the hand closest to it.
- ◆ Ask your friend to release your dog.
- ◆ Keep pointing until your dog picks a bowl.
  You might have to call your dog by name.
- ◆ Repeat the test a few times.
  Change which bowl hides the food.
- ◆ How often does your dog get the right answer?
  Is your dog guessing, or communicating?

Try these things to see what happens:

- ◆ Stop pointing as soon as your dog is released.
- ◆ Hold your dog while your friend gives the signal.
- ◆ Use a different signal:
  - • Change the distance between your finger and the bowl.
  - • Point with your opposite arm, across your body.
  - • Instead of pointing, nod your head or stare at the correct bowl.
- ◆ Test a different breed of dog. German shepherds and border collies are bred to work for people. Does this make them better communicators?
- ◆ Use a toy instead of a treat. What information, other than communication, might your dog be using to find the food?

CHAPTER 4

THE SECRET OF SOUNDS

Imagine a wolf on a hill at night. She raises her muzzle to the moon and . . . barks?

This makes no sense, right? Wolves are known for howling, not barking. They only bark when attacking or defending themselves. But domestic dogs bark in many situations. Some dogs rarely stop! This change happened sometime during domestication.

Scientist Svetlana Gogoleva says, "It's impossible to compare the vocal repertoires of dogs and wolves. They've been different animals for thousands of years. To see how domestication affects animal sounds, we needed to compare at the earliest stages. Foxes," Gogoleva explains, "have only been domestic for 50 years. In this case, domestic foxes are priceless."

Howling helps wolves communicate with their packs.

DIFFERENT BARKS, DIFFERENT MEANINGS

Dogs bark in so many situations that scientists once thought barks had no meaning. They did not think dogs were trying to communicate.

To test if barks contained information, scientists recorded dogs in different situations. They measured the loudness and deepness of each bark. They also measured how long dogs waited between barks.

The recordings showed that bark sounds changed in different situations. When dogs defended their owners, their barks were harsh and close together. Dogs paused between each bark when they were locked up alone. Barking sounds were higher when dogs played. Because barks have different sounds, they might have different meanings.

Like dogs and foxes, domestic cats and guinea pigs make different sounds than their wild relatives.

A German shepherd learns how to protect its owner from attackers.

For communication to happen, people would have to understand these meanings. The scientists asked people to listen to recorded barks. Then people had to match each bark to a situation. In one test, people got it right up to 80 percent of the time.

The scientists then asked people to match the bark to a feeling, like happiness, anger, or loneliness. Most picked the right feeling, even if they had never owned a dog.

Scientists now believe that dogs bark to communicate. They think communication works because feelings change human voices and dog voices the same way. This helps dogs and people recognize each other's moods. It explains how dogs convince people to play with them. It also explains how dogs know we are mad when they chew up our homework!

Two foxes ignore each other during Gogoleva's experiment.

Gogoleva's team designed an experiment to understand the sounds foxes make. They compared the sounds of 25 domestic foxes and 25 aggressive foxes. The scientists recorded over 25,000 noises, and found eight different sounds. All foxes whined, mooed, and growled when they saw people. Aggressive foxes also snorted, coughed, and barked. Domestic foxes did not. They cackled and panted instead. Aggressive foxes never made those sounds around people.

Different human words mean different things. Was that also true for foxes? To find out, Gogoleva's team needed to know why foxes used each sound. They built a special cage with three sections. They put a fox in each end. Foxes could choose to stay at their own ends. Or they could go into the middle section and meet.

THE DNA FOR SOUNDS

Domestic foxes communicate with people by moving their bodies in certain ways. They open their mouths, wag their tails, pounce, and roll over. Domestic foxes also allow people to pet them, something aggressive foxes never do. In 2011, Anna Kukekova's team found instructions in fox DNA that linked to domestic behaviors. Now they are looking for DNA linked to domestic sounds.

The foxes ignored each other most of the time. When they did meet, they were sometimes angry and sometimes playful. Foxes with different feelings made different sounds.

Then the scientists compared sounds made by domestic foxes and aggressive foxes. It did not matter whether foxes were domestic or aggressive—they talked to other foxes the same way. In this case, the foxes' feelings were more important than their ancestors.

These foxes are feeling playful.

These foxes feel angry with each other.

Gogoleva's experiments used two kinds of foxes:

- Domestic foxes that were bred for tame behavior
- Aggressive foxes that were bred for mean behavior

Each kind of fox could have two kinds of feelings:

- friendly and playful
- angry and mean

Svetlana Gogoleva stands outside a fox's cage during her experiment.

Talking to People

Gogoleva wanted to understand how foxes felt about people. She designed another experiment to find out. The scientist chose 15 domestic foxes and 15 aggressive foxes. Then she stood in front of each fox's cage. The foxes could see her, but not touch her. For five minutes, Gogoleva recorded the sounds each fox made.

Gogoleva's team measured how many sounds each fox made every minute. Aggressive foxes talked at the same speed for all five minutes. They coughed and snorted, whined and mooed. The types of sounds did not change. In Gogoleva's first experiment, foxes had used these same sounds to say they were angry with each other.

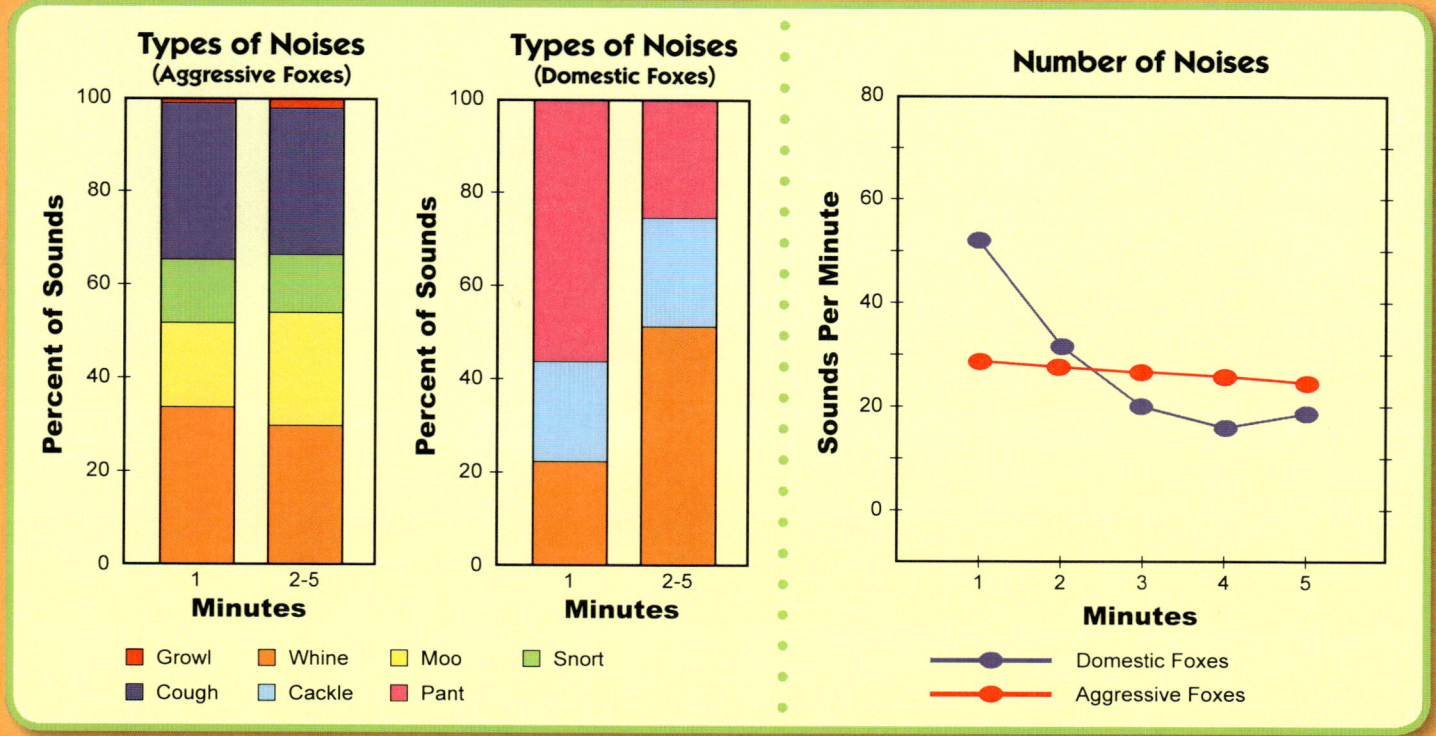

Types of Noises (Aggressive Foxes)

Y-axis: Percent of Sounds (0, 20, 40, 60, 80, 100)
X-axis: Minutes (1, 2-5)

Types of Noises (Domestic Foxes)

Y-axis: Percent of Sounds (0, 20, 40, 60, 80, 100)
X-axis: Minutes (1, 2-5)

Number of Noises

Y-axis: Sounds Per Minute (0, 20, 40, 60, 80)
X-axis: Minutes (1, 2, 3, 4, 5)

Legend:
- Growl
- Cough
- Whine
- Cackle
- Moo
- Pant
- Snort

- Domestic Foxes
- Aggressive Foxes

Domestic foxes were different. For the first minute, domestic foxes made lots of noises one after another. Then they started to pause between each sound. At first, domestic foxes made more pants than any other sound. After one minute, they made fewer pants and more whines. From her first experiment, Gogoleva knew foxes used these sounds when asking each other to play.

Swift foxes and arctic foxes are wild relatives of red and domestic foxes. In the wild, swift and arctic foxes cackle to communicate with their mates and puppies.

Domestic foxes love attention from people!

Speaking the Same Language

Gogoleva's experiments proved that domestic foxes and aggressive foxes have different feelings about people. Aggressive foxes want to attack people, so they make angry sounds. Domestic foxes love people. They use friendly sounds to ask people to play.

When domestic foxes first see people, they explode with sounds. Many sounds, one after the other, usually mean animals have very strong feelings. This is important for communication. Scientists think repeated noises tell animals to pay attention, and to keep paying attention. In the case of domestic foxes, attention from people is exactly what they want!

In nature, only young wolves and foxes play. Gogoleva says, "There is clear proof that domestication makes adult dogs and foxes act like puppies around humans." When asking for playtime, though, foxes have an advantage over dogs. Their cackles and pants sound a lot like human laughter. When making these sounds, foxes and humans both have partly-open mouths. Gogoleva thinks this is why it's so easy for humans and foxes to communicate.

Can you spot Chaser in this pile of her toys?

When they are happy and playful, foxes' and people's faces look the same.

CHASER'S TOYS

How many human words can a dog understand? Chaser, an American border collie, holds the record. In three years, scientists John Pilley and Alliston Reid taught her the names of 1022 different toys.

To prove Chaser knew these words, the scientists kept her in one room. In a second room, they placed 20 toys. Pilley and Reid told Chaser to fetch a certain toy. Because the toys were in a different room, it was impossible to cheat. Chaser fetched the right toy at least 18 times out of 20.

The scientists wanted to know how Chaser learned. They put a brand new toy in a room with seven toys Chaser already knew. Next, they asked her to fetch, using a new word for the new toy. Chaser chose the right toy every time.

To do this, Chaser used fast mapping. This is a type of educated guess. Scientists believe human children also use fast mapping to learn new words.

CHAPTER 5

MEET THE FOXES

Every year, more domestic foxes are born than scientists need for experiments.

At first, extra foxes went back to fur farms. Now foxes are so tame that Belyaev's team sells them as pets!

Two Americans, Renée Baker and Mitchel Kalmanson, are the scientists' partners. They help the foxes find new homes. In February 2012, Baker and Kalmanson brought Anya home to Michigan in the United States. By 2013, they had delivered foxes to owners in Germany and the Netherlands. People in France, the United Kingdom, Mexico, Spain, and Russia will also have fox pets soon.

Three foxes live with Baker and Kalmanson in Florida. Each fox is different.

On airplanes, foxes travel in this special cage. It has dishes for food and water. A tray underneath is lined with baby diapers. That makes the cage easy to clean during the trip.

Dante tries to steal a girl's shoelaces.

Dante

Dante is a silver-black boy. He is playful and curious. Dante tugs your hair, your sleeves, and your shoelaces. He steals your gloves right off your hands. When he drops them in his water bowl, he looks like he is laughing.

Pusha hiding under her litter box.

Pusha

Pusha is a girl fox with platinum fur. She is the smallest and a bit of a bully. She chases and shoves the other foxes. When she is really angry, Pusha hides in her kennel and squawks. She sounds like an old lady scolding rowdy kids.

Prada in the sunshine.

Prada

The third fox, Prada, is also a platinum girl. She is quiet and sweet. Prada was invited to a party once. She sat in the birthday girl's lap for two hours.

Arsi

Arsi has red fur. He lived with Baker and Kalmanson before finding his human family. Dante, Pusha, and Prada love Arsi. When he visits, they quickly start a game of tag. The four foxes dodge and weave and twist and jump. They chase each other in circles and even climb the fence. Like dogs, they crouch and pounce. They roll over to show their bellies. At the same time, they are quick and agile like cats.

The playing foxes are also very noisy! But they do not sound like dogs. They sound like geese, or a pack of monkeys chattering. It is clear the foxes have fun together.

Arsi, Pusha, and Prada playing tag.

"Foxes are good-tempered creatures, as devoted as dogs but as independent as cats, capable of forming deep-rooted pair bonds with human beings."
—Scientist Lyudmila Trut, 1999

Arsi and Prada dancing.

Arsi chases Dante through a tunnel.

Owning A Fox

Foxes need the same kinds of food and medicine as dogs. They need harnesses and leashes. But for many people, foxes would make very bad pets. Baker says, "These foxes are like border collies. They need a job." Like border collies, the foxes are smart, get bored quickly, and have lots of energy. If they do not have enough to do, they get into trouble.

Arsi's mom, Carol Price, knows this is true. One of Arsi's games is burying each of his toys in a separate hole. Then he digs them up and switches them around. Arsi does not live indoors, because he puts everything in his mouth. Like all domestic foxes, he loves to tug and chew. Plastic water bottles are a favorite toy, but he crushes them in minutes. His owners have to make sure he does not eat them.

Domestic foxes are happiest living outside. But they need special pens. The fences must be very deep. Arsi's mom says, "He digs holes with his paws faster than I can dig with a shovel." It would be very dangerous for these foxes if they escaped. Many people think wild foxes are pests, like rats or pigeons. They do not know about domestic foxes. Domestic foxes look a lot like wild ones. If a domestic fox got out, someone could hurt or kill it. That person would never know the fox was a pet.

The Future of Foxes

Scientists made foxes domestic so they could learn about dogs. Already, foxes have answered many questions about dog domestication. They have shown scientists how domestic animals communicate. And one thing the foxes keep saying is how much they love people.

Domestic foxes are here because of people. It is our job to make sure they have safe and happy lives. As long as we do, we will continue to learn from them. And the foxes will continue to talk.

"There is something moving in the emotions of these foxes, that at the sight of even a strange person, they try actively to attract attention with their whining, wagging of tails, and specific movements."
— Dmitri Belyaev, 1979

Pusha and Dante wrestling.

HOW TO BUY A FOX

Step 1: Find Out If Foxes Are Legal

Many governments do not understand that Belyaev's foxes are domestic. They think the foxes are wild animals. Special laws control who can own a fox and where the fox can live.

It is illegal to bring a domestic fox into Canada. No one can keep a fox as a pet. These laws will not change until governments understand that foxes are special.

To help, you can write to the Canadian Food Inspection Agency. Explain how domestic foxes are different from wild foxes. Ask the government to change the laws. Visit this website to find out how:

Canadian Food Inspection Agency
www.inspection.gc.ca/animals/terrestrial-animals/imports/policies/live-animals/pet-imports/ferrets-etc-/eng/1331923269633/1331923405610

Step 2: Learn How To Take Care Of A Fox

Domestic foxes are special animals that have special needs. Before you buy one, learn everything you can about taking care of foxes. Here is a good place to start:

The Domestic Fox
www.domesticfox.com/#!care

Step 3: Contact Featuring Animals

If a fox is the right pet for you, write to Renée Baker and Mitchel Kalmanson through their website. They will answer your questions and help you get your fox!

Featuring Animals
www.featuringanimals.com

In the United States, every state has different laws about foxes. Contact your state government to learn the rules about foxes where you live.

FURTHER INFORMATION

In the Library

De la Bédoyère, Camilla. *100 Things You Should Know About Dogs & Puppies*. Broomall, PA: Mason Crest Publishers, 2011.

Kalman, Bobbie. *How Do Animals Communicate?* New York: Crabtree, 2009.

Love, Ann, and Jane Drake. *Talking Tails: The Incredible Connection Between People and Their Pets*. New York: Tundra Books, 2010.

Markle, Sandra. *Foxes*. Minneapolis: Lerner Publishing, 2010.

Myers, Jack. *How Dogs Came From Wolves, and Other Explorations of Science in Action*. Honesdale, PA: Boyds Mills Press, 2001.

Simon, Charnan. *Wolves*. New York: Scholastic, 2012.

Featuring Animals
www.featuringanimals.com
Want your own pet fox? Visit this
website to find out how to get one.

Volodins:
Bioacoustic Group Homepage
www.bioacoustica.org/index_eng.html
Click "Mammals Sound Gallery," and
then "Carnivores." On this page you will
find the sounds of the red fox.

Fox Behavior
http://cbsu.tc.cornell.edu/ccgr/behaviour/
Fox_Behavior.htm
This website includes videos of fox
behavior, and information about fox DNA.

YouTube Channel for Anya
www.youtube.com/user/BlondeHusky?
feature=watch
This is the YouTube channel for Anya,
the first pet fox in North America. "Anya
vs. Cockroach" is super cute!

Duke Canine Cognition Center
http://evolutionaryanthropology.duke.
edu/research/dogs
This website has information on
Brian Hare's research on canids and
communication. Find out how your dog
can join experiments!

An Australian shepherd dog looks at a red fox.

GLOSSARY

aggressive:
foxes that snarl, snap, and attack when they see humans. Scientists bred aggressive foxes from wild ones, and they are the opposite of domestic.

ancestors:
an animal's parents, grandparents, great-grandparents, and so on, going back through history.

breeding:
pairing male and female animals to get them to mate and have babies.

canine:
a family of dog-like animals that includes dogs, wolves, foxes, jackals, and dingos.

communication:
using sounds, body movements, facial expressions, or written words to share information.

descendants:
an animal's children, grandchildren, great-grandchildren, and so on, going into the future.

DNA:
a molecule in living things that affects an animal's looks and behavior.

domestication:
a type of evolution that begins with wild ancestors and ends with their tame descendants.

evolution:
a natural process that causes changes in a species' DNA. Evolution takes many years and helps species survive in new living conditions.

fast mapping:
fast mapping is a mental process that helps people and animals guess what a word means the first time they hear it.

object-choice experiment:
a test of whether animals understand human pointing. The scientist points to one of two bowls and lets the animal choose between them.

pack:
a group of wolves, usually family members, that live and communicate with each other.

socialization period:
the amount of time a baby animal has to form good feelings toward other animals. The feelings can be for the animal's family, or for another species, such as humans.

species:
a group of living things that can mate with each other, and have characteristics in common. Giraffes, eagles, and carrots are all examples of species.

train:
to teach an animal to follow commands or behave in a specific way.

vocal repertoires:
all of the sounds that a species can make.

ABOUT THE AUTHOR

L. E. Carmichael

L. E. Carmichael has a PhD in wildlife population genetics and has published children's science books on everything from gene therapy to hybrid cars. She read a paper about domestic foxes in 1999, and has been waiting for a chance to write about them ever since.

Visit Lindsey online at www.lecarmichael.com

ABOUT THE PHOTOGRAPHER

Brian Dust

Brian Dust grew up catching frogs and chasing lizards. These days, he prefers fuzzy animals to creepy crawlies. If a fox would have fit under his jacket, he would have smuggled one home.

THE PUBLISHER

Ashby-BP Publishing

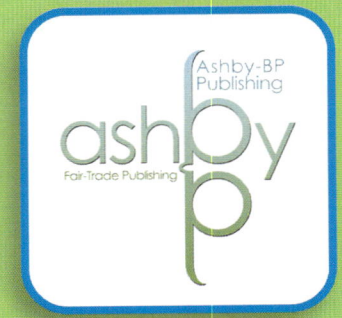

What do ethics have to do with book publishing?

Ashby-BP Publishing is the first Fair-Trade Book Publisher. We believe purposeful ethics are key to a revitalized book industry. Fair-Trade Publishing seeks to ensure everyone involved in the process – from writer to designer to bookstore – has their needs met. Why? The old model doesn't work anymore.

The world's biggest publishers have long bemoaned their loss of market share and reduced profits. In response, they consistently laid-off editors, designers, reduced royalties to writers, forced many writers to pick up promotional costs, and raised the list prices of their titles.

It didn't stop there. The same major publishers made deals with online giants and large book store chains, with crippling effect on libraries and independent book stores. As a result, readers now receive lower quality titles but pay more for them, more mid-list writers live in poverty than ever before, countless over-qualified literary and design professionals are now unemployed, and an increasing number of libraries and independent book stores close forever each and every day.

Fair-Trade Publishing, also called **Ethical Publishing**, means *seeing the bigger picture first*.

A Fair-Trade Publisher knows the livelihoods of all involved in the book market are interdependent; we need each other. We consider everyone's needs in the publishing process and work to fulfill them. For example, we collaborate with writers rather than dictate terms. Or, in the case of retailers, we work with them to make the book buying process as risk-free as possible, and actively promote their locations. We're also flexible enough to change with the needs of our partners. It only makes sense.

We believe happier literary professionals produce higher quality books, which make for more satisfied readers. And if making money at the expense of others' needs becomes obsolete, then selling overpriced books becomes a thing of the past.

Isn't this what we all want?

What do ethics have to do with book publishing? Everything.

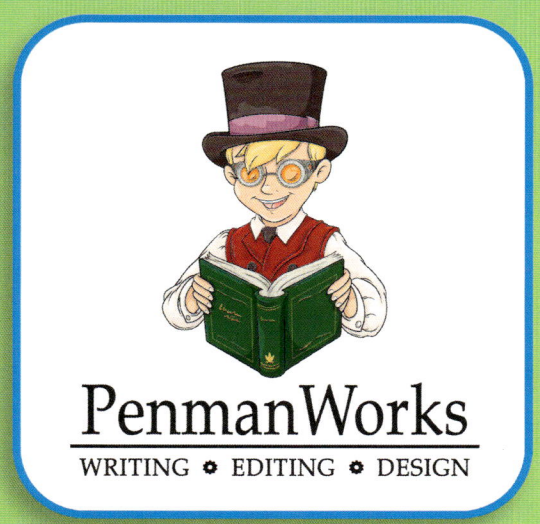

PenmanWorks

PenmanWorks is an innovative writing, editing, and design company focused on children's publishing. Specialties include picture books, nonfiction titles, elementary education products, and comic books.

Founded by renowned children's book veteran, Michael Penman, our background includes 15 years' of industry experience, 32 books in print, 50+ publishing awards, co-development of the *Adventures of Riley* children's brand, and a proven commitment to our clients and their project goals.

Clients and partners have included Scholastic, McGraw-Hill, the Smithsonian Institution, SmartLab Toys, KCTS9/PBS, Jack Hanna, becker&mayer, BrightStart Learning, SimplyFun Games, Cornell Labs, World Wildlife Fund, and the Wildlife Conservation Society.

INDEX

PHOTO/ILLUSTRATION CREDITS

Photo Credits:

Front cover: Arsi close-up © L. E. Carmichael. Page 1: Arsi and Prada together © Brian Dust. Page 2: Pusha and Dante playing © Brian Dust. Page 4: Arsi and Pusha playing © Brian Dust. Page 5: Three wolves in the snow © Dennis Donohuek/Shutterstock Images; BW Belyaev © Ria Novosti/Science Photo Library; Arsi licking © L. E. Carmichael; Dante and Arsi fighting © L. E. Carmichael; Arsi and the girls © L. E. Carmichael; Australian shepherd with red fox © Eric Isselee/Shutterstock Images; Fox pup © Featuring Animals. Pages 6-7 (spread): Boy teaching puppy to sit © Crystal Kirk/Shutterstock Images. Pages 8-9 (spread): Three wolves © Dennis Donohuek/Shutterstock Images. Page 9: Fox skull closeup © Maher et al. (2011) PLoS One 6:e15815; BW grave shot © Davis and Valla (1978) Nature 276:608-610, courtesy of François Valla. Page 10: Snarling wolf © Tom Tietzk/Shutterstock Images. Page 11: Puppy licking girl © Jesse Kunerthk/Shutterstock Images. Page 12: Wolf white background © Iakov Filimonov/Shutterstock Images; Bulldog white background © Willee Cole/Shutterstock Images. Page 13: BW Belyaev © Ria Novosti/Science Photo Library; Three pups on a couch © Svetlana Gogoleva. Page 14: Black fox pinned ears © Svetlana Gogoleva. Page 15: Full body black fox back of cage © Ilya A. Volodin; black fox relaxed ears © Svetlana Gogoleva; Prada looking scared © L. E. Carmichael. Page 16: Red pup in wooden box © Featuring Animals. Page 17: Arsi wearing harness and kissing © L. E. Carmichael. Page 18: Two girls with golden retriever © Martin Valigursky/Shutterstock Images. Page 19: Snarling fox © Rob Kemp/Shutterstock Images. Pages 20-21 (spread): Arsi licking © L. E. Carmichael. Page 22: Dante and Brian's hand © L. E. Carmichael. Page 23: Puppy being bottle fed © Sergey Lavrentev/Shutterstock Images; White pup with black markings © Svetlana Gogoleva. Page 24: Dante and girl communicating © L. E. Carmichael. Page 25: Boy with dog © Nikole Penman; Girl with dog © Neil Bjorklund. Pages 26-27 (spread): Wolf howling © Cynthia Kidwell/Shutterstock Images. Pages 28-29 (spread): German shepherd attack training © Marcel Jancovic/Shutterstock Images. Page 31: Arsi pawing Dante © L. E. Carmichael; Dante and Arsi in the water bowl © L. E. Carmichael. Page 32: Svetlana outside a cage © Svetlana Gogoleva. Page 33: Arctic fox © Jean-Edouard Rozey/Shutterstock Images; Swift fox adult and pup © Colette3/Shutterstock Images. Page 34: Renee and three kids holding Prada © L. E. Carmichael. Page 35: Laughing girl holding Prada © L. E. Carmichael; Chaser with mound of toys © Robin Pilley. Page 36: Cage with main door open © L. E. Carmichael. Page 37: Dante goes after shoelaces © L. E. Carmichael. Page 38: Pusha hiding under the litter box © L. E. Carmichael. Page 39: Prada in the sun © L. E. Carmichael. Pages 40-41 (spread): Arsi and the girls © L. E. Carmichael. Page 42: Arsi and Prada dancing © L. E. Carmichael. Page 43: Arsi and Dante in the tube © L. E. Carmichael. Page 44: Arsi close-up © Brian Dust. Page 45: Arsi's belly rub © L. E. Carmichael. Pages 46-47 (spread): Dante and Prada through tube © L. E. Carmichael. Pages 48-49: Girl hugs Prada © Brian Dust. Page 50: Border collie on playground © Olga_i/Shutterstock Images. Page 51: Australian shepherd with red fox © Eric Isselee/Shutterstock Images. Page 52: Fox pup © Featuring Animals. Page 53: Prada and Pusha relaxing © Brian Dust. Page 54: Author L. E. Carmichael holding Prada © Brian Dust. Page 55: Photographer Brian Dust playing with Pusha © L. E. Carmichael. Page 60: Prada ready to play © Brian Dust.

Illustration Credits:

Page 22: object choice experiment © Jody Bronson, Phobaphobia Productions
Page 30: cage with three compartments © Jody Bronson, Phobaphobia Productions
Page 33: types of calls made each minute © Gogoleva et al. (2011) Behavioural Processes 86:216-221

Disclaimer: Every effort is made to ensure that all photo captioning and credit information is accurate and up-to-date. If you think we have incorrectly identified an image or subject, please notify the author or publisher. Model releases are on file for all applicable shots.

Photography used with permission by: Colette3, Crystal Kirk, Cynthia Kidwell, Davis and Valla, Dennis Donohuek, Eric Isselee, Iakov Filimonov, Ilya A. Volodin, Jean-Edouard Rozey, Jesse Kunerthk, L.E. Carmichael, Maher at al. (2011) PLoS One 6:e15815, Marcel Jancovic, Martin Valigursky, Ria Novosti/Science Photo Library, Rob Kemp, Robin Pilley, Sergey Lavrentev, Svetlana Gogoleva, Tom Tietzk, Willee Cole, Shutterstock.

Interior Illustrations by Michael Penman/PenmanWorks and Jody Bronson, Phobaphobia Productions.

Cover and Interior Design by Michael Penman/PenmanWorks, www.PenmanWorks.com

Indexed by Dan Connolly, www.wfwbooks.com

An Ashby-BP Imprint
Alberta, Canada
California, U.S.A.
http://www.ashby-bp.com

ISBN-10: 0988163853
ISBN-13: 9780988163850
BISAC: JUVENILE NONFICTION/Foxes/Dogs/Wolves & Coyotes/ Pets
         JUVENILE NONFICTION/Science & Nature/Experiments & Projects

Further information about this book can be found at http://www.ashby-bp.com

Printed in The United States of America

CPSIA information can be obtained
at www.ICGtesting.com
Printed in the USA
LVXC01n1637041213
363882LV00022B/409

* 9 7 8 0 9 8 8 1 6 3 8 5 0 *